A Love Not Forgotten

By Linda Shenton Matchett

A Love Not Forgotten

By Linda Shenton Matchett

To

The millions of Land Army girls and others

Who did their bit on the home front during

World War II

Prologue

Perspiration trickled down the sides of Chaz's face as he gripped the letter and stared at the looping script on the page. Not that he had to read the words. He had memorized them months ago. The two-year-old paper crinkled in protest as he tightened his hold.

January 1944

Dear Chaz:

The moon is full and lights up my room with an eerie blue glow. It's nearly three o'clock in the morning, and I've barely slept. I miss you desperately. What are you doing? Are you safe? Are you looking at the moon, too? Today's casualty list included two more lads from the neighborhood. Giles and Vincent Thompson. Can you believe it? Two different battles, but they are both gone. Mrs. Thompson is beside herself with grief.

Mother says I should only send you cheerful, newsy letters, but our relationship is deeper than that. We've always been able to talk about everything, the good and the bad.

Food is dearer than ever, so even if one has points for an item, it's impossible to find. But I shouldn't complain, since you are probably eating tinned meat and haven't seen a fresh vegetable since you went away.

Work is good. I enjoy what I do, although I can't tell you anything about it. All very hush-hush. But as much as I love my job, I love you more, and I can't wait to become your wife.

There. I've said it. I want to marry you. I know you didn't propose before you left, because you didn't want me to feel beholden, but that doesn't change how I feel. I'll wait for you forever. Hurry home, my darling.

Your best girl,

Allison

A LOVE NOT FORGOTTEN 2

"Chaz! I've been looking for you. Are you going to sit out here all day?" The sound of boots crunching on the gravel grew louder as the owner of the voice approached. "You'll be fried to a crisp."

Shoving the missive into his pocket, Chaz turned toward the voice and squinted at the figure hurrying across the circular driveway.

"Come inside and have some tea." Hospital orderly, Ian Kellogg, had to shout to be heard over the thundering surf. "The quack said sunshine would do you good, but you're already red as a beet. Besides, you can't avoid the lads forever."

Chaz bit his lip. Forever. *She* said she'd wait forever. But who was she?

Ian's shadow blocked the sun's glare. Hands on his hips, he tilted his head, his usual mulish expression painting his face. "We'll play chess. You like that."

"Don't coddle me. And I'm not avoiding the lads."

"Sure, you're not. And I'm Princess Elizabeth."

Heaving himself to his feet, Chaz stiffened his spine. The scar tissue on his back pulled against the healthy skin and shot knife-like pain across his shoulders. He winced and swayed against the chair. He was lucky. At least he hadn't lost a limb or damaged his face during the plane crash.

A crash he didn't remember.

Chapter One

Allison White eyed her ivory-gowned image in the mirror and grimaced. "The war is over. How can we be worse off than before it started?"

"Because we do not get as many clothing coupons as we did during the war. You already know this." Rosa Quincey adjusted Allison's sleeve and smiled. "I do not want to make you sad, but you did a wonderful job updating your mother's wedding dress."

"That's okay, Rosa. They're never far from my thoughts although it's been six years since they were killed during the Blitz. I'd like to think they're watching from heaven. You and Basil were so kind to let me live with you."

Rosa shook her head. "It is not kindness. I love you very much, my friend. And speaking of love, Don is so in love with you he would marry you wearing your Land Army uniform."

Sighing, Allison twirled until she faced her friend, the floor-length silk dress rustling as she moved. She lifted the skirt to reveal black, peep-toe shoes. Holding out one foot, she wiggled her toes. "I can't believe I broke the heel on my white, coupon-buster shoes. These look terrible."

"We will find you some to borrow, *ja*? The girls on the farm will ask their friends and we will find your size."

"Guess that will take care of my 'something borrowed.' We still need to find something blue."

Rosa dug into her pocket. "I have waited to give this to you." She withdrew a hair-comb studded with blue crystals and handed it to Allison. "Victory rolls are going out of style, but perhaps you could wear your hair in a chignon."

Allison's eyes welled with tears. "It's gorgeous. Where did you get it?"

"That little dress shop on High Street. Mrs. Kensington got them from her cousin in America. They are just paste, but rather pretty."

"You didn't need to do that. Having you as my matron of honor is enough."

Rosa shrugged. "You were the only one who befriended a poor, German girl in the middle of a war. That deserves a gift."

Waving her hand in a dismissive gesture, Allison snorted. "The other girls didn't know what they were missing by shutting you out."

"You always did take up for the…how do you say it…little dog?"

Allison smiled. "The underdog."

"*Ja,* the underdog. Anyway, no more talk of the past. Sweet William and phlox should be in bloom by your wedding day in May. Carnations, too. We will fill the church, and it will be beautiful."

Allison's chest tightened. She pivoted back to the mirror and rubbed her hands against the dress's satiny smooth material. Leaning closer to her reflection, she studied her face. Did her wan complexion betray her feelings of confusion and second thoughts?

"Are you thinking about Chaz, Alli?"

A frown creased Allison's forehead. That answered the question about whether anyone could tell she wasn't sure about marrying Don.

"Talk to me." Rosa patted the yellow quilt-covered bed. "If you cannot share your deepest thoughts with your best friend in the privacy of your bedroom, where else can you do it?"

Allison tugged at the neckline. "First, help me out of this thing."

"Gladly." Rosa unzipped the dress, and Allison stepped out of the garment and grabbed her dressing gown from the upholstered chair in the corner. Putting on the gown, she cinched it around her waist. The plush material of her wedding dress swished and whispered as Rosa hung the handkerchief-hemmed, lacy creation in the oak wardrobe.

Allison dropped onto the bed. The springs groaned, and she bit back a groan of her own. What had she gotten herself into?

The door to the wardrobe closed with a bang. Rosa sat down, and the bed complained again. Allison arranged her dressing gown over her legs and drew her knees to her chest.

"You are doing the right thing." Rosa spoke softly. "You will not forget Chaz and you always love him, but it was two years ago his plane was lost. Even when it is hard, you must go forward, and Don is a good man; he loves you."

"I've loved Chaz for as long as I can remember. I can't simply set that aside. Is it fair to marry Don when I still love Chaz?"

"Do you think I have forgotten Conrad or that I have stopped loving him?" Rosa's voice caught. "I love Basil very much, but I will always miss my gentle, kindhearted Conrad. He was my life, and is still in my heart."

Allison squeezed Rosa's hand. "I had no idea, Rosa. I thought you put all that behind you."

"Never. And you will not either. Conrad is part of me, and Chaz will always be part of you, but you cannot cut yourself off from loving others. Don is different than Chaz, but he is just as special. He will provide for you and care for you." Rosa's eyes narrowed. "Have you shared your concerns with him?"

"He's been away in Scotland on business. He's constantly away." Allison's shoulders slumped. "Maybe that's for the best."

Rosa shook her head. "Nonsense. When does he return? You need to discuss your concerns with him before it is too late."

"He'll be back on the twentieth of May."

"Ten days before the wedding." Rosa nudged her. "Let us pray about this. God knows your heart and Don's. He wants what is best for you both. I am a living testament to that. If someone had told me I would fall in love, have children after being barren for a decade during my first marriage, and become a well-known member of the community, I would have laughed."

"I've prayed until I'm hoarse. God doesn't seem to speaking to me at the moment."

Rosa tilted her head. "Or he could be telling you to wait."

"Wait for what?"

"For whatever mysterious plans he has for you."

Chapter Two

Voices bounced off the walls in the cavernous dining hall as Chaz hunched over his tea cup and inhaled the steaming amber liquid.

"Milk, Chaz?"

Chaz shook his head. During the war he had learned to drink tea without the creamy additive. That much he could remember. The pitcher passed in front of him as his table-mate handed the vessel to the man on his left.

"Not very talkative today, eh, Chaz?" Ian nudged his shoulder.

Shaking his head again, Chaz continued to stare into his cup. Why had he agreed to come inside? The lads meant well enough, but they seemed to take it as a personal affront that he didn't want to chatter or laugh at their inane jokes.

He sighed. Pressure had begun to build behind his eyes, the pain always came without warning. Rubbing his forehead, he willed the throbbing to go away. Sometimes it lasted as long as two or three days, but generally the pounding receded in a few hours. The docs told him the headaches were a result of the head injury he sustained in the crash.

"A headache, is it?" Ian's voice was soft near his ear.

Chaz shrugged. Ian was a good chap, but he was as bad as a mother hen, fussing over him. Chas guzzled the tea and put down the cup with a thunk. The delicate handle cracked and came off in his hand. The voices at his table stilled.

"Sorry. I, uh, didn't mean to do that." He stood and yanked on his cuffs to straighten his sleeves, then smoothed his jacket and dipped his head. "Please, excuse me."

Without waiting for a response, he threaded his way between the chairs and escaped through the doorway. He ducked down the corridor to his right and out the front door. The sun struck his face, and shards of pain exploded in his head. Moaning, he stumbled. His hand caught the wall, and bending at the waist, he sucked in the stifling, hot air and coughed.

Hands supported him around his shoulders, and he sagged against the figure.

"You're a stubborn man, Chaz. You know I don't think any less of you because of your headaches, don't you?" Ian chuckled. "You make my father, the general, seem like a kitten. There's a bench a few yards away. Can you make it?"

Swallowing against the nausea that threatened to return his tea, Chaz nodded and allowed Ian to guide him onto the wooden bench where he slumped with his head in his hands. "Thank you."

"You're welcome." Ian sat too, stretched out his legs, and crossed his arms. "It seems the doctors are no closer to determining the cause of your headaches or finding a cure. Do you think you should seek help elsewhere? Perhaps in London?"

"Dr. Bosworth and Dr. Taunton can't agree on the problem. Bosworth surmises that there is physical damage to my brain, but Taunton believes it is psychological. He wants me to see a therapist."

"Psychological? That's ridiculous." Ian scowled. "How can it be psychological when you have amnesia?"

"He espouses some theory that the subconscious mind can impact the conscious mind, and the two are fighting which causes pain."

Ian snorted. "Does he have any proof of that?"

"I have no idea." Chaz eased himself upright. The horizon swayed and tilted, then steadied. A slight breeze caressed his cheeks, and the thrumming in his head receded. He blew out a breath and turned to his friend. "But he might be right. I've noticed a pattern."

"That's great, Chaz." Ian clapped him on the back, and Chaz grunted.

Ian flushed. "Sorry, old chap. I got caught up in the excitement."

Chaz chuckled. "You always do."

"What's this about a pattern? Have you told either of the quacks? What do they think about this?"

"Easy. You're the first to know." Chaz nibbled on his lower lip. Would Ian think him a wimp if he voiced his fears? Would he finally remember who he was? Or would he remain a man without an identity?

Ian gripped Chaz's shoulder. "You can tell me anything. We've been through a lot together these last two years you've been at the hospital. Do you think I would betray your secrets? Your uncertainties?" He lowered his head to meet Chaz's eyes. "But if you can't tell me, you can always take it to God."

"Like he cares." Chaz scowled. "If he did, he wouldn't have allowed me to crash and lose my memory."

"He let you live, my friend. That trumps anything else."

Chaz swept his arm toward the towering brick building then back at himself. "You call this living? I don't know who I am. I have one name, and that's only because of this letter." He pulled the page from his breast pocket. "Fortunately it was packed in my waterproof kit bag or it would not have survived. No one can determine who I am. I was found without identity discs or any other means of identification. The military seems to think I somehow went off course, because no missions had been flown anywhere near where I was located. My family, wherever they are, has no idea if I'm dead or alive. And this woman is obviously important to me. But who is she? There's no envelope, no return address. Am I to live forever as a mystery?"

Chaz shoved the letter back into his pocket and clenched his fists. His heart threatened to burst from his chest. Closing his eyes, he took a deep breath. If only one other person could understand the depth of his anguish and confusion. Ian couldn't. *His* girlfriend married him days after he returned home, and now there was a baby on the way. *He* was able to move on with his life.

"I know you don't want to hear this, Chaz, but God knows who you are, what you've experienced, and the extent it has affected you, even if the rest of us don't. And despite what you think, he has the situation under control. We don't always understand his plans, but he has his reasons for allowing this to happen."

Swallowing against the lump in his throat, Chaz frowned, unwilling to speak. If only what Ian said was true.

"Take things one day at a time. Talk to the doc about the pattern you think you've recognized. See what he says." He squeezed Chaz's shoulder. "And keep reading that letter of yours."

Chaz's face warmed, and he sighed. "Maybe you're ri—"

"Chaz! Chaz Powell, is that really you?"

His head whipped around toward the voice.

A burly, dark-haired man wearing the white uniform of a hospital orderly waved as he trotted toward them. The man pumped Chaz's hand, a deep laugh rumbling in his chest. "I'd know you anywhere. How are you, mate?"

His surname was Powell? Chaz's mouth opened and closed several times as he stared at the man, looking for a feature he recognized: Closely cropped beard that covered the lower part of his face; hair shorn in a crew cut. Did the man truly know him?

Ian stuck out his hand. "Ian Kellogg. I'd say you're an answer to prayers, my friend. How do you know our man, Chaz?"

"Giles Finlay." Giles shook Ian's hand then offered his hand to Chaz. "Lieutenant Powell was part of my squadron. We lost him during a sortie over Berlin." He turned to Chaz. "You had some engine trouble and disappeared into the clouds on the way back, so we thought your plane went into the Channel. A search was done, but it didn't turn up anything. What happened? How did you get here?"

Chaz shrugged. "I must have gone off course. A Danish fisherman found me in the North Sea clinging to a floating piece of airplane wreckage with a gaping head wound and burns on my back. He was part of the Resistance, so he used his network to get me to England. I didn't know who I was. My identity discs were missing, but I was carrying a letter that told me my first name. My uniform gave them my rank."

He looked at Ian. "I was treated at a couple of different places and finally transferred here. They won't discharge me because I continue to suffer excruciating headaches. Until you showed up, I didn't know my last name."

Giles cocked his head. "Well, isn't that something? I've heard of guys who've lost their memories, but I've never met one." He peered at Chaz. "So, you don't recognize me? Do you remember anything about our flying together or the war?"

"Not one moment."

Ian gave Chaz a one-armed hug. "We have to advise the administrator. He can notify your family that you're alive." He poked Chaz's pocket. "And soon, you'll meet the young lady in that letter."

Allison raced up the porch steps of Rosa's house. Her ragged breath caught in her throat as she sagged against the doorframe. She had run most of the distance from her home, and her legs trembled from the exertion. Wiping the wetness from her cheeks, she read the telegram once more.

The door opened and Rosa stepped out, her brow furrowed. "Mrs. Powell called saying you were on your way and you would explain. What is going on? Are you all right?"

Sobbing, Allison fell into Rosa's arms and was wrapped in a warm hug. Minutes passed before her cries abated. She sniffled and extricated herself. "Chaz is alive."

Rosa's eyes widened. "It is a miracle, *ja*. Praise God! Where is he? Is he coming home? How did you find out?"

Allison held up the crumpled telegram.

With an arm around Allison's waist, Rosa drew her inside. "You must be stunned. Come in, and I will make some tea. You can tell me everything."

Once in the living room, Allison sank back against the plush, forest-green sofa and closed her eyes.

"Rest." Rosa patted her shoulder. "I will be back with our tea." Her footsteps receded, and Allison took a shuddering breath.

A cabinet door banged, and the clink of china sounded from the kitchen. Moments later the kettle whistled, and Rosa returned with a tray filled with prepared tea. She handed Allison a delicate, pink-floral porcelain cup. "Just the way you like it."

Allison held the cup near her nose and inhaled deeply. "You make the best tea in London. How is that possible? You're not even English."

"*Mutti* Noreen taught me." Rosa smiled. "Now, enough stalling. Tell me about Chaz."

"I came here immediately after receiving the telegram. It was sent to his parents, and they delivered it to me." She smoothed the paper on her knee. "The War Department is pleased to inform you that Lieutenant Charles Powell, formerly reported dead, is alive. He is currently somewhere on the south coast. More information to follow."

"That is wonderful."

"Is it?" Allison stuffed the document into her handbag. "Why didn't the Army know where he was? Is he hurt? Are they going to send him home?" Tears flooded her eyes. "Does he still love me?"

"Of course, he does."

"Then what do I do about Don?" She met Rosa's gaze. "I'm supposed to marry him next month."

Chapter Three

Smoke belched from the locomotive's chimney as it pulled into the station. Standing on the platform, Chaz cleared his throat and squared his shoulders. His stomach tingled as if filled with a swarm of bees. He pressed his hand against his middle to quell the sensation. Clouds of noxious fumes swirled amidst the crowd, and he wrinkled his nose. The cacophony of voices blended with the clatter of doors slamming and porters tossing luggage onto the train.

Hands stuffed into his pockets, Ian jabbed Chaz with his elbow. "I'd forgotten how loud civilization can be. You'll miss the peace and quiet of the hospital more than you think."

"I already do." Chaz's gaze swept the mob. "People are apparently making up for their lack of travel during the war. Maybe I'll ask to accompany the bags."

Ian snorted a laugh. "You may want to rethink that. A pair of goats was led onto one of the freight cars."

Chaz gave an exaggerated shudder.

"Besides, you don't want to mess up that spiffy, blue suit the hospital administrator gave you."

"All aboooaaaaarrrrd!"

"It's time, Chaz." Ian extended his hand. "Keep in touch. It won't be the same without you."

Chaz shook Ian's hand and smiled. "I have no doubt you'll find someone new to torment. I'll write once I get settled."

"I'll hold you to that. Now, hurry onto the train before we get maudlin."

Chaz nodded and picked up his valise. He squeezed Ian's shoulder with his other hand then climbed into the train. He walked the aisle searching for a seat. Finding a vacancy near the front of the car, he sat down with a sigh and looked out the window. Ian was gone, engulfed in the chaos.

He felt someone sit beside him and cringed. Would he be stuck with a chatterbox for a seat mate? The ride was several hours. Better to get introductions over with. He turned and blinked several times.

A young woman dressed in a lilac-colored suit looked at him with a smile. She gripped a small, patent-leather handbag in her gloved hands. A dainty, white hat perched at a jaunty angle on her raven-black hair.

"I, uh—" Chaz coughed. "I'm Charles Powell."

"Nice to meet you, Mr. Powell. My name is Mariana Ulster."

"Please, call me Chaz."

"Chaz? An unusual nickname. How did you come by it?"

Perspiration broke out along his hair line. What should have been an innocuous conversation was already taking a difficult turn. Should he make something up? No. He might be angry at God for allowing the accident and subsequent amnesia, but he wasn't a liar.

"If it's an embarrassing story, don't feel you need to share it." Mariana's crystal-blue eyes crinkled in the corners as she grinned at him. "I didn't mean to pry. Hazard of the trade-I'm a journalist."

Chaz widened his eyes. "A journalist? For a newspaper?"

"Yes. When the lads went off to war, lots of jobs opened up. When they came home, I was pushed aside, but by then I had lots of experience under my belt. The smaller papers are more willing to hire a woman. I did some stringer work for a while, and then the *Hackney Herald* picked me up."

"What did you cover during the war?" Chaz's breathing evened out. The conversation had shifted from him for the moment.

"London. I was there for the Blitz."

Her eyes took on a faraway look, and his heart tugged. What horrors had she survived? "That must have been frightening. You seem to have survived all right."

"I did, but several of my friends weren't so lucky." Her lower lip trembled. "And I lost my brother at Dunkirk."

"I'm sorry for your loss. How difficult for you."

"Yes, but my faith sustains me during the hard times. My parents are struggling with his death. He was their only son. But lots of families can say the same thing. Let's hope the world never has to suffer another war."

"Amen to that." He pointed to her bag. "Where's your typewriter? Don't reporters have to carry one?"

Her face lit up, and her eyes sparkled. "Only stringers do that. The office provides machines for employees. I can't imagine having to haul one with me, although the correspondents did during the war."

Chaz massaged the tightness in in neck. "Do you notice how our conversation keeps turning back to the war? Certainly there must be something more pleasant we can discuss."

The whistle shrieked, and the train lurched forward. A porter stopped beside them. "Tickets, please."

Chaz handed his ticket to the man while Mariana rummaged in her bag. After much searching, she found hers. The official punched their stubs then returned them before moving down the aisle.

Mariana stuffed the scrap of paper into her handbag. "I'm going home. How about you?"

"Me, too." He took a deep breath. There was no way around it. If they were going to converse, he couldn't avoid telling her about the amnesia. "I was a pilot with the RAF and crashed a couple of months before Normandy. Fortunately the fisherman who found me was part of the Resistance. He and his wife smuggled me to England."

"And you're all right, now?"

"I've got scars on my back that periodically give me discomfort, and the occasional severe headache, but otherwise, no lasting physical damage." He scrubbed at his face. "However, I lost my memory in the crash. I found out my identity a few days ago when one of the lads from my unit transferred into the facility where I was staying. The docs are hoping my memories will come back if I'm in familiar surroundings."

Her brow wrinkled. "They may be right. I did an article a few months ago about the psychological effects of the war. I interviewed some men who suffered from amnesia and recovered after going home."

"That's all well and good for them. But I'm not giving myself any false hope."

She stared at him for a long moment. "Don't you want to remember?"

He shrugged.

Turning toward him, Mariana crossed her arms. "Seems like there's more to your story than you'd like me to know. Who doesn't want to regain their memory? Perhaps you're afraid of what will happen if you do."

He bolted upright. "I'm not afraid. If you must know, I'm angry. Angry that God allowed this to happen. What sort of God takes a man's memories?"

Mariana shook her head. "God didn't take them, the war did. Look, I don't understand why certain things happen. Why did my brother have to die? I don't know and probably never will. God has his reasons for what he does. But if you keep blaming him for something he didn't do, you're going to become a bitter young man. That's a terrible way to live."

"A friend of mine gave me a similar speech not too long ago." Chaz snorted a harsh laugh. "Guess I need to give it some thought."

Her cheeks reddened. "I apologize if I've offended you. Would you like me to find another seat?"

He rubbed his forehead. "No, don't do that. I'm the one acting like a heel. I'm sorry." Running a finger around the neck of his shirt, he swallowed. It was a wonder she hadn't slapped him for his behavior.

"How about if we agree to talk about something else."

She laid her hand on his arm. "Sure, but I hope you will give what your friend and I have said some thought."

His arm tingled where the warmth of her hand seeped through his sleeve. God certainly wasn't pulling any punches by using a pretty girl to get his attention.

———◆———

Chaz stared out of the window as the train shimmied and swayed on its approach to the station. Green and blue blurs solidified into trees, meadows, and sky, and jagged, white clouds hung above the landscape. Pressure on his shoulder confirmed that Mariana still slumbered. Carefully avoiding any discussion of God, their conversation had ebbed and flowed as the miles passed. After a filling meal in the dining car, they had returned to their seats and she had drifted off to sleep about an hour ago.

Crowds milled about on the platform. His palms slicked. Would he recognize his parents? Would incidents from his past flood into his brain?

Would he ever remember the man he was? He searched the faces ogling the train. No one looked familiar.

Brakes squealed and metal screeched as the locomotive pulled to a stop. Mariana sat up, and he pivoted toward her. "Welcome back, sleepyhead. We've arrived at our destination."

She settled her hat on her head and smiled. "I must look a fright. You were quite gallant to let me use your shoulder, especially after having just met."

"I'm happy to be of assistance." He touched his forehead in a mock salute. "May I help you with your bags?"

"Thank you, but my father is meeting me and has probably already lined up a porter. Besides, you have a family of your own to meet. You can't put it off forever, you know." She held out a small card. "I wish you the best. If you need me, I can be reached through the newspaper."

"You're very kind."

Knocking sounded on the window behind him. He turned to find a man and woman with salt-and-pepper hair beaming at him while a young, blonde woman at their side waved, a shy smile on her face. All three had tears coursing down their cheeks, their mouths forming words he couldn't

hear through the glass.

"Do you recognize them?" Mariana's voice was low and close to

his ear.

His stomach tightened, and he shook his head.

Now what?

Chapter Four

Allison paced in front of the shelves that lined the food storage room at the Quincey farm. The space was bigger than most kitchens. Generous to a fault, Rosa had sent her to select several jars of canned goods to take with her to the Powell's home.

What had she been thinking when she agreed to have dinner with Chaz and his family? She was engaged to Don. Was it appropriate to visit her former fiancé?

Don would understand. Wouldn't he?

She rubbed her forehead then picked up a jar of green beans. Too much thinking was giving her a headache. There would be other visitors at the house. Lots of Chaz's friends had been invited to celebrate his return to life. No one would notice she was there.

Yeah, right.

He may not remember her or their relationship, but he had failed to hide his appreciation of her face and figure when he alighted from the train yesterday, flushing to the roots of his hair when she caught him staring. Polite as always, he stammered an apology and said it had been months since he last saw a woman in street clothes.

The air in the car had bristled with tension and uncertainty on the drive to Rosa's with the Powells. Mrs. Powell had clung to Chaz's arm and cried; Mr. Powell had gripped the wheel in silence, periodically swiping away the tears; any time her arm had brushed against Chaz he flinched as if he'd been burned, and he didn't speak more than a dozen words during the entire ride.

"What am I doing?" She set the jar back on the shelf with a bang. "I'm going to call Mrs. Powell and cancel. A night on the couch with a good book is in order, not an awkward meal with a man who can't remember me."

"You will do no such thing."

Allison whirled, her cheeks warm.

Rosa stood in the doorway with her arms crossed. "I wondered what happened to you."

"I'm trying to talk sense into myself. Dinner with Chaz and his parents is inappropriate. I'm marrying Don."

"But it seems you might still love Chaz, *ja?* You have a decision to make." Rosa walked over to the shelves and placed four jars into the basket on the floor. "But not tonight. It is a welcome home party for a hero. Basil and I will be there, as will many of Chaz's friends. You cannot change your mind this late."

Allison slumped against the wall. "Everyone will be watching us, gauging our interaction."

"I will be right beside you the entire night." Rosa pulled Allison into a warm hug then turned her toward the door. "Now, go get ready. Wear Chaz's favorite outfit. Maybe that will help him remember."

<hr>

Three hours later, Basil's black, Ford sedan pulled to a stop in the circular driveway of the palatial Powell home. Despite the warmth in the car, Allison shivered. Rosa patted her arm then lifted the basket of canned goods from the floor and climbed out of the vehicle. Allison took a deep breath and followed her. They trailed Basil up the wide staircase of the limestone manor house. Soft amber light streamed from several windows, giving the mammoth home a welcoming glow.

"A year after the war's end, and I am still not used to seeing houses lit at night." Rosa spoke in a whisper.

Basil rapped twice on the heavy, mahogany door. "The war scarred us in many ways, my dear."

The door opened and the Powell's butler, Meeks, bowed in the doorway. "Good evening. The family is expecting you, sir." His voice rumbled in his chest.

He swept his arm toward the interior of the house, and the trio stepped inside. Rosa handed him their offering of food, and he set it on a small table in the foyer. "Thank you, Mrs. Quincey."

They walked down the hallway behind Meeks, his limping gait a reminder of a bombing raid in Hastings halfway through war. He opened the door to the drawing room, and Allison searched the faces for Chaz.

About two dozen people milled around the ornate room. The Powells came from old money and had lost very little during the conflict.

Chandeliers sparkled from fifteen foot ceilings, and the Queen Anne furniture had been pushed against the wallpapered walls to make space for the crowd. An oil painting of Chaz and his parents watched the gathering from above the tiled fireplace.

Mr. Powell clapped his hands, and the buzz of conversation ceased. "Mr. and Mrs. Quincey, welcome. And Miss White, we're so pleased to have you grace this room with your presence again, as you have so many times in the past."

Allison's face warmed and her heart skittered, but Chaz stared at her from the far corner, his face devoid of emotion. In the past, Chaz would have swept through the crowd taking her elbow and whispering in her ear, "You wore that dress because it's my favorite." Why had she allowed Rosa to talk her into coming?

The silence stretched awkwardly until Mr. Powell cleared his throat. "Yes, well. Now that everyone has arrived, dinner may be served."

Meeks slid opened the carved panel doors that led to the dining room. Soft music played from the Victrola. China, crystal, and silverware gleamed on the mahogany table. Flames flickered and danced on the ivory tapers in the eight-armed candelabra as visitors checked place cards and

seated themselves.

Mrs. Powell gestured to one of the chairs. "Allison, you're on this

side between Chaz and Mrs. Quincey."

Her stomach quivered. She should have known Chaz's mother

would push them together. Allison's gaze shot to Chaz, who stood frozen

next to his father. She gave him a faltering smile and walked to the chair.

"Thank you, ma'am. You're most kind."

"Mother, I asked you to seat Miss White away from me." Chaz

scowled. "I'd appreciate it if you would give me the courtesy of granting

my request."

Chapter Five

The following morning, Allison and Rosa sauntered along the path circling a small pond in the center of town. Rosa pushed the perambulator that held her son, Conrad. Named in honor of her first husband, the toddler gripped a wooden, toy train in his fist and looked at his mother, with serious eyes. His straight, dark hair spiked up in numerous directions.

Sunshine warmed Allison's back, and she waggled her fingers at Conrad. His gaze slid to her face. His forehead wrinkled before he looked away.

Allison laughed. "He's a determined little thing, isn't he?"

Rosa leaned toward the carriage and made kissing noises at Conrad. He giggled and waved at her.

"Mostly with people he does not know. Perhaps you should spend more time with him."

"What I know about babies fits on the head of a pin. I don't think that's a good idea."

"I would not leave you alone." Rosa bumped Allison's shoulder with her own. "You must learn about children sometime if you plan to be a wife and mother."

Allison licked her dry lips. "About that…" She ran her hand through her hair. "Last night was a disaster."

"*Nein,* it was not as bad as all that. You handled yourself with grace, which is more than I can say for Chaz."

Her eyes filled, and Allison blinked away the moisture. "Maybe so, but I was mortified. I wanted to leave, but to do so would have embarrassed his parents. You saw how stilted the conversation was. Most of the guests spent the evening watching Chaz and me. It was all I could do to choke down the meal. Chaz didn't even do that. He pushed food around on his plate and then left when the sweet was served."

"His parents should have reprimanded him."

"You can't blame them. He's a grown man and causing a scene would only create more fodder for those who love to gossip. I'm sure it won't be long before stories begin to circulate." She yawned. "Needless to say, I didn't sleep well. Despite my best efforts to forget what happened, the evening replayed in my mind most of the night."

"You poor dear." Rosa gave her a one-armed hug. "Yet despite Chaz's behavior, I sense you still care for him. You recognize, as I do, that his acting as he did was perhaps out of anger for his situation. Is marrying Don the right thing to do when you are so confused about your feelings for Chaz?"

Seating herself on a small bench near the water's edge, Allison rubbed her chest. "Chaz and I had something special. I thought he was the one. Do I turn my back on that?"

Rosa dropped down beside her. Conrad fussed, and she rocked the carriage in slow, even motions. He snuffled and closed his eyes.

"Have you prayed about marrying Don?"

"I—"

A steady tapping sounded behind them, and the women turned toward the clatter. Dressed in a black suit and wearing a straw boater, a twenty-something young man walked the path on a pair of crutches, the left leg of his trousers pinned up above the knee. He dipped his head in greeting and continued on his way.

Allison stared at his retreating back. Conrad cried out, and she turned back toward the pram. Rosa laid the boy on his stomach and patted his back as she whispered into his ear. When he seemed to nod off, she leaned back on the bench.

"That man…he was a soldier, wasn't he? I wonder how he feels about losing his leg for King and country. Do you think his physical loss is easier than Chaz's psychological loss?" Allison pointed to the man's distant figure.

"Each case is different, Allison. Some of the men who came back have moved on with their lives, adjusting to their injuries as best they can. Others, not so much. Chaz is just as much a casualty as those with physical wounds. In some ways, he is more handicapped than they are. I cannot imagine what it is like for him not being able to remember anything. I would much rather experience the pain of losing my husband, than not to have the memories of our life together."

"Does it still hurt very much?"

"Have you forgotten your own grief when you thought Chaz was dead two years ago?"

Allison shook her head. "No, but Conrad's been gone nearly twelve years. That's a long time."

"Not as long as you might think. Sometimes the sorrow is as fresh as if he died yesterday." She grasped Allison's hand. "Most days I rest in the blessings God has given me: Basil, little Conrad, *Mutti* Noreen, and you."

"Basil is a special man. I saw that when I first went to work for him during the war. He treated the Land Army girls like family. Not all employers were like that. Before I came to Basil's farm, I worked for a man north of London. He was surly and vindictive. Most girls put in for a transfer within days of arriving. You'd think the Ministry of Labor would notice."

"Perhaps." Rosa shielded her eyes with her hand, squinting at two men across the pond.

"What is it?" Allison glanced at the pair. "Who are they?"

"Basil, but I do not recognize the other man." Her mouth closed in a firm line.

"Why does that upset you?"

"He said he was going into the city for the day, yet here he is. Why would he lie to me?"

Chapter Six

Murky sunlight seeped through the pre-dawn haze. Despite the early hour, the day already promised to be hot and humid. Chaz sat in the small, wooden boat across from his father. Their fishing poles dangled over the edge of the craft.

Chaz yawned, and his jaw popped. "Remind me why we had to come out before the fish woke up."

His father chuckled and reeled in the line. "So we could be here when they're ready for breakfast."

Chaz's stomach rumbled, and he grinned. "Is it too soon to dig into whatever Mum packed for us?"

"If I know your mother, she packed enough for breakfast, lunch, and tea. Perhaps more."

"She's made it no secret she plans to fatten me up."

"Like a Christmas goose. Isn't that what she said last night?" Dad cast his line over the water, and the sinker cut through the surface with a resounding plop. "She's happiest when she's feeding those she loves."

Laying his fishing rod in the bottom of the boat, Chaz opened the wicker basket and pulled aside the blue-checked towel that covered the contents. "Judging from the amount of food in here, she must be ecstatic." The yeasty aroma of fresh bread mingled with the sharp fragrance of hard-boiled eggs. He opened a small jar and inhaled. "Mmm. Black Currant jam."

Dad pointed to a jar in the bottom of the basket. "Orange marmalade, too. And if I'm not mistaken, she's included tomatoes, fruit salad, several kinds of cheese, baked beans, and sausages. All your favorites."

Chaz froze, and he swallowed against the lump in his throat. "At least someone knows what my favorites are. I've been eating hospital mush and pudding for two years and haven't had any way of knowing what I like."

Silence hovered over the tiny boat for a moment, then Dad gripped Chaz's hands with his warm, calloused fingers. "Son, I can't begin to imagine what you are experiencing. You must be frightened, angry, confused, and hurt all bundled together, fumbling through each day wondering who you are, then suddenly being identified by someone you have no recollection of knowing. Now, you're living with strangers because you can't remember us either. It's not been easy for you."

Chaz yanked his hands away and wrapped his arms around his middle. "You're right. No one can possibly know what it's been like for me. It took months for me to recover from a crash I have no memory of. I underwent multiple surgeries while in hospital to fix the damage to my back, and I still suffer headaches—headaches so severe I wonder if I can hold down more than a menial job."

He sighed. "There's a young woman whom I loved at one time, but whose face means nothing now. And why can't I remember you or Mum, or the home I grew up in? I still get lost upstairs. How is that possible? I spent twenty-five years in our house, and in the blink of an eye, it's as if I never lived there."

"Mum and I have been praying for you; praying that you'll adjust no matter what happens."

"Bah! A lot of good that will do. God is the one who allowed this to happen in the first place. Why would he choose to heal me? This is obviously his idea of a grand old joke."

Dad sat back as if slapped, then shook his head. "That's your anger speaking." He sighed. "You may not want to hear this, but you accepted Christ as Savior in your life when you were a lad of eight. Before you left for the war, you were even considering a call to the church."

Chaz's eyes widened, and he raked his hand through his hair. "That's not going to happen now."

"With God, all things are possible. He can choose to return all your memories, or he may decide that it is best that you begin creating new memories from this moment forward. We can't understand his plans, but he truly wants what is best for you."

"How can you say that after all that has happened? You thought I was dead, causing unnecessary grief. How is that best?"

Dad smiled, and his eyes welled with tears. "A part of us died when we thought we lost you, but the church surrounded us in love during that awful time. They supported us physically, emotionally, and spiritually. And as we healed, we were able to minister to others."

"Like pawns in some cosmic game of chess."

"No, like a family. We are brothers and sisters in Christ, and we serve each other as needed." Dad cleared his throat. "Son, in one sense you have been given an amazing gift. You can't remember your childhood or your call to the ministry, but you also can't remember the regrets from your former life either. As someone who made more than his share of poor choices, I'm somewhat envious." His face brightened. "The Bible says we are new creatures in Christ. Old things have passed away. You're a brand new creature with a clean slate. Was God's plan simply for you to come home and start a new life? Or perhaps your return was to give Allison the peace she needs to marry Don Laird. You can choose to turn your back on God and allow your feelings to fester until you become a bitter man, wallowing in hatred, or you can choose to embrace your future and all the potential it holds."

Dropping his gaze, Chaz studied his hands. *God, are you out there? I don't know what to do.*

"Come to me, you who are heavy burdened. I will give you rest."

Jerking up his head, Chaz looked at Dad. "Did you hear that?"

"Hear what?"

"I heard a voice that said 'Come to me, you who are heavy burdened. I will give you rest.'"

Shaking his head, Dad said, "I didn't hear anything, but that doesn't mean the voice wasn't real. God speaks to us when we call out to him."

The tightness in his chest eased, and Chaz slumped on the hard, wooden seat. Tears gathered, and he pressed his palms against his eyes to stem the flow. He bit back a sob that forced its way from his mouth. Would Dad think him weak? Chaz couldn't seem to stop the emotions overtaking him.

Dad drew Chaz into his arms. "Son, no matter what society says, it is a strong man who cries, especially when coming face to face with his Savior. I'm here for you, and we'll tackle whatever happens together."

Chaz crumpled against Dad, his agonized cries howling across the
water.

Chapter Seven

Allison washed dishes in the sink while Rosa wiped down the counters. The tangy, sweet fragrance of allspice hung in the kitchen air, and a warm breeze fluttered the dotted Swiss curtain.

Blowing out a breath, Allison grimaced. "It's terribly hot to be baking today, but the thought of another dinner without a sweet depresses me. Mrs. Fisher gave me her eggless sponge recipe at church last week, and it seemed like a good day to make a go of it."

"It smells divine. The end result will be worth a bit of suffering in the heat."

"After so much rain, sunshine should be considered a blessing, but the temperature is sweltering. Makes me want to have a lie down."

Nodding, Rosa pressed the back of her hand against her forehead. "After the cake comes out of the oven, we should reward ourselves with a dip in the pond, *ja?* It is Saturday, the chores can wait a bit longer."

Allison drained the sink and dried her hands before dropping into one of the vacant chairs. "I can't remember the last time we had such a hot day in April. What is the weather like in Germany?"

"I lived in Berlin. July is our warmest month, but nothing like this." She smiled. "Enough chit-chat. You have been avoiding the subject of your upcoming marriage since you came home. Have you been praying about the situation?"

Rubbing at a scratch on the table, Allison shrugged. "I can't seem to form the words because I don't know what to ask."

"I understand. It was like that for me when Conrad died. I was a believer, but my grief was so overwhelming, all I did was cry when I prayed." She laid her hand on Allison's arm. "What is your heart telling you?"

"That I need to break off my engagement with Don. He deserves someone who can love him completely, not as a consolation prize. That's no way to start a marriage. Even if Chaz and I don't rekindle our relationship, I can't marry Don." Her lower lip trembled. "I hate the idea of hurting him. And what about all the people who have been invited to the wedding? Won't they be angry that I'm returning their gifts?"

Rosa grinned. "They might be angrier if you kept the presents." She sobered. "Honestly, it does not matter what they think. I learned that from *Mutti* Noreen. It is more important that you are doing what is right in God's eyes and going where he leads you. Yes, Don will be hurt, but as with the story of Joseph and Mary, we can pray that God will speak to him. We can also pray he finds the woman of God's choosing."

"I need to tell Don straightaway, but it feels wrong to telephone him while he is away on business. Wouldn't he rather hear from me in person?"

"Perhaps, but that is not possible. I will sit with you when you make the call, and I think tonight is not too soon."

Tears trickled down Allison's cheeks. "If it's the right decision, why does it hurt so much?"

"Because you love him, although not enough to be his wife. And regret is a painful emotion."

Allison sniffled. "How did you get to be so wise, Rosa?"

"I have walked through my own dark valleys." She gestured out the window where Basil walked the potato fields, periodically crouching to inspect a plant. "I wonder if another valley is coming in the near future. He has lied to me, or so it seems. Why would he tell me he had an appointment in London, only to be seen talking with a stranger in town? Twice I have started to confront him, but each time I could not bring myself to follow through."

She shook her head. "Does Basil regret marrying me, a penniless widow from a foreign country? Like you, does he love someone else? Would he tell me if he did?"

Drawing Rosa into a hug, Allison stroked her back. "We'll get to the bottom of this. There has to be an explanation." *Please, God, let us know what it is. And give me the right words when I speak to Don.*" She sighed. It was going to be a long night.

Chapter Eight

Two days later Chaz and Allison sat on a worn, woolen blanket on the banks of the pond on Basil's property. The water shimmered in the sun, and a tepid breeze stirred up white caps on the surface. A fish jumped sending a trio of turtles hurtling off their floating log with a loud plop. Moments later their reptilian heads poked into the air like periscopes as they swam back to the limb.

Chaz chuckled. "Tenacious little things, aren't they? They seem quite put out by the inconvenience of having tumbled into the drink."

Allison nodded then ducked her head.

He reached to take her hand, then pulled back. Taking a deep breath, he licked his dry lips. "Thank you for your willingness to see me. I was a boor at the welcome home party, and I'm sorry. I hope you'll forgive me."

She looked up, an uncertain smile on her face. "Of course, I forgive you. That's what Christians do, but I'm struggling to understand why you acted as you did."

His face warmed. "You're right, but unfortunately even the doctors don't agree about why I have the mood swings or how to treat them. They've said it's something I may have to deal with for the rest of my life."

"That must be difficult for you."

"Some days it's worse than others." Stretching out his legs, Chaz propped himself on his elbow. Needles of pain stabbed his back, and he winced.

"Are you all right, Chaz?"

"Just a bit of discomfort. Nothing I can't handle." Picking up the brown bottle next to his plate, he pulled out the stopper and took a swig. He needed to lighten the mood, or he would scare Allison away. She still seemed skittish, despite his apology. "This is excellent ginger beer. Where did you get it?"

"Basil has been producing his own since '42. He had trouble finding any he cared for, so he tried his hand at making it. Rosa says he won't drink anyone else's."

"Does Basil succeed at everything he touches?"

Allison shrugged. "He does seem to have a keen mind." She took a bite from her cucumber sandwich.

Chaz rubbed the hollow of his back with a fist. "The man seems to have prospered even during the war."

"Basil was too old to serve in combat, but he did what he could. For one thing he employed dozens of Land Army girls on his farm during the war. Rosa and I both worked for him, but Rosa's employment ended when he proposed marriage to her."

She plucked at the blanket. "The Quinceys have such a romantic story: A poor despised immigrant widow and a rich landowner. It was love at first sight. Rosa had accompanied her mother-in-law, Noreen, back to England from Germany, and they arrived with barely two shillings to rub together. When Rosa first started working on the farm, her English skills were limited and many shunned her for being German. But I saw her humble persistence in taking care of Noreen, and we became friends."

"A romantic at heart, aren't you?"

"Yes, and it was fun to be part of their courtship. None of the other girls would speak to her, and in fact, many were downright hostile. During the war, most people lumped all Germans together as Nazis." She shook her head. "But Rosa was so quiet and sweet. Maybe I was naïve, but I never suspected her of agreeing with Hitler's philosophy."

Naïve was right. His stomach churned. She had no idea how clever the Nazis were, how they infiltrated villages and organizations in order to ferret out information and those they felt were traitors to the Reich. He'd heard stories from the lads at Highlands.

His forehead wrinkled in a frown, and he yanked the stopper from the bottle. Eyeing her over the bottle, he took a gulp. He wiped his mouth with the back of his hand still glaring at her. "Of course she would act pleasant. If spies and infiltrators were rude and disruptive, no one would be taken in by their subterfuge. I suppose it's good she turned out to be genuine." He tilted his head. "Have you always been so trusting?"

Her smile faltered, and he berated himself. With a few words, he had once again hurt Allison. He didn't deserve her friendship.

"Yes, I have. It's one of the things you used to tease me about while we were…er…together. As a matter of fact, you used to go out of your way to take advantage of my gullibility." Smoothing out the blanket, she poked her finger through a small hole in the fabric. "You and my brother, Lloyd, made it a point to outdo each other with your tricks."

"That wasn't very sporting of me, was it?" He continued to frown. "Why ever would you be my girl, if I treated you like that?"

"Because it was all in good fun; because you cared about my thoughts and feelings. You took me seriously when the other lads in our class didn't." She met his gaze. "You were a kind and decent man, Chaz. You still are."

He shook his head. "How can you say that? You don't know me." He barked a harsh laugh. "*I* don't know me. The war robbed me of my memories. Perhaps it also robbed me of my charming personality."

Sitting up, his scars pulled, and he swore.

Allison gasped, and her face pinked. The ugly word hung in the air between them as his gaze pierced hers.

"See? Not so captivating and appealing now, am I? I'm not the man you once loved, nor will I ever be. I suffer debilitating headaches and excruciating periods of dark moods the doctors can't seem to cure. It's best you're engaged to marry someone else, someone undamaged by the blasted war."

He struggled to his feet and stood with his hands on his hips. "In fact, why are we here? How would your fiancé feel about our little tête á tête? This is entirely inappropriate. You should never have agreed to see me when you're walking out with another man." He stalked toward the water. Shoving his hands into his pockets, he stood with his back to her, his shoulders hunched.

She walked toward him and stopped a few feet behind him.

"I'm no longer engaged, Chaz. I broke it off with Don. But even if I hadn't, you and I were friends before we fell in love. Good friends. Friends who stood by each other no matter what." Her voice broke.

"That's why I was willing to join you today. I thought you could use a friend."

He spoke over his shoulder. "I don't need your pity. Stop feeling sorry for me and go home…please. I just want to be left alone."

Chapter Nine

Allison stifled a sob as Chaz continued to stand with his back to her. Overhead, a raven screeched. In the distance, an answering shriek echoed. She looked up. Gray clouds had gathered, blocking the sun. The warm fingers of the earlier breeze turned into frigid needles. Thunder rumbled, and the skies opened.

Within moments, her hair was plastered to her head. She wiped her eyes and squinted through the downpour. Chaz still stood at the water's edge, his shirt drenched and adhering to his thin frame.

Allison rushed to his side and tugged at his arm. "I'll leave you alone later. Right now, we need to pack up the picnic and get out of this storm.

He looked at her, his eyes blank.

What was wrong with him? Didn't he hear her?

She grabbed his hand and yanked him toward the blanket, raising her voice over the pelting of the rain. "Help me put away the food before it all washes into the pond."

Chaz blinked several times then seemed to focus on her face. Swiping at the water streaming down his face, he nodded. Allison dumped the half-eaten food into an empty bowl and bundled it in a towel while Chaz shoved plates, silverware and serving utensils into the wicker basket and slammed the lid. She picked up the blanket and rolled it into a ball.

He grabbed the handle of the basket with one hand, and they staggered toward the small gazebo perched on a rise about thirty yards from the pond, their muddied shoes slipping and sliding across the sodden ground. Allison stumbled as her saturated skirt flapped and tangled itself around her legs.

They clambered up the steps, their feet thudding against the wooden treads. Once under the roof, Allison dropped the blanket, and Chaz set down the basket. Grinning, he shook his head back and forth, spraying droplets all over her.

Allison caught a glimpse of the old Chaz, and her heart skittered. She had done the right thing in breaking her engagement with Don. He had taken the news over the telephone as well as could be expected, wishing her the best and claiming he understood—although the coolness in his voice told a different story. But even if she and Chaz never married, she knew without a doubt that he was her only love. Anyone else was second best.

Biting her lip she blinked back the tears that threatened to course down her face. She would have blamed the rain for the moisture on her face, except that her nose and eyelids reddened when she cried—and Chaz knew it.

His dark mood seemed to have lifted for the moment. Would it return? Forcing a laugh, she pushed him away. "Stop! You're getting water all over me."

"I don't see how I could make the situation worse. You couldn't possibly get any wetter." He put his left arm around her waist, and grabbed her hand with his right. Pressing her against him, he tucked her head under his chin. "Dance with me."

She tried to pull away, but he gripped her tighter. Her breath caught, and she whimpered. Did he know how his nearness affected her?

<hr/>

Chaz hummed Dorsey's *I'm Getting Sentimental Over You* and led her around the floor. Allison struggled for a moment, then seemed to acquiesce and leaned against him. Did she realize how pretty she was? Not just her porcelain skin and shining, blonde hair, but the beauty in her soul. She saw the good in everyone, even him, a broken-down, used-up former soldier. Giving of herself, she was gracious and kind. He may not remember her, but since his return her goodness had started to chip away at the hard shell around his heart.

What would life had been like without the war? Would he have entered the ministry like his father suggested? Proposed to Allison? Her letter indicated the war was the only thing that stopped him from asking for her hand.

He reached the end of the song, and they stopped moving. Releasing her, Chaz stepped back. With a finger, he raised her chin until they were looking eye to eye. She seemed to search his face. His gaze dropped to her lips, his heart thudding in his chest. What would she do if he kissed her? Would she think this was simply another mood swing? He had to chance it. ,

Thunder clapped, and they leapt apart. Allison's face flushed, and she bent to pick up the blanket. Folding it, she avoided his gaze.

His palms slicked, and perspiration trickled between his shoulder blades. "Allison, I'm sorry. I'm not sure what came over me."

"It's fine. There's no need to apologize." Although the blanket was as drenched as her clothes, she hugged it to herself.

"I was out of line. I didn't mean to take advantage of your hospitality. It won't happen again."

"I said it's fine. Nothing happened." She dropped the blanket onto the floor and stooped to open the basket. Rearranging the jumble of dishes and food, she said, "We'll wait out the storm, then head back to the house. I'm sure Noreen can find some dry clothes that might fit you. One of the farm hands must be your size."

Chaz squatted in front of her and reached into the basket to still her hands. "Look at me."

"I can't." Her voice caught.

"Can't or won't?"

"Does it matter?"

He swallowed against the lump in his throat. She had every right not to trust him. "To me it does." He squeezed her fingers. "Have you always been this stubborn?"

She yanked her hands from his. "Yes. You said it was one of the things you loved about me."

"You wouldn't lie to me because I can't remember, would you?"

She gasped. "Chaz! What a thing to say."

"I have to joke about my amnesia, or I get angry. The docs said it's a coping mechanism."

"How do you feel about that?"

He shrugged. "Honestly, I'm not sure. But I had a long talk with Dad, and he feels I've been given an opportunity for a fresh start."

"That's a wonderful way to look at your situation." She cleared her throat. "Your mum indicated you are angry with God, so you might be offended to know that Rosa and I made a pact to pray for you. We love you as a Christian brother, and want to see you at peace about this."

He hung his head. "I don't understand how you can be nice to me after the chaos I've caused. I've ruined your life, first as someone presumed dead, then as the chap who broke up your engagement. I don't deserve your kindness."

"Frankly, I think my broken engagement is a blessing in disguise. I was having second thoughts long before you reappeared. As for my kindness, it's what friends do for one another." She took his hands in hers. "How about if we take things one day at a time?"

"You've got yourself a deal." He sighed. *Lord, I'm going to need your help here. She doesn't realize that some days it's all I can do to get through one hour at a time.*

Chapter Ten

As the sun dipped below the horizon, Rosa and Allison settled on a bench in the flower garden behind Rosa's stone farmhouse. Conrad slept in Rosa's arms, his head nestled in the crook of her neck. Every so often, the toddler would snuffle in his sleep.

Allison stroked Conrad's downy, soft hair. Sighing, she crossed her arms. "That's a beautiful sunset. It makes today's rain a distant memory."

Rosa's eyebrow arched. "You have been sighing on and off since Chaz left wearing castoffs from one of the farmhands. Are you ever going to tell me about your picnic?"

"I haven't been as transparent as all that, have I?"

Snickering, Rosa nodded. Conrad mumbled in protest then settled again with a quiet sigh.

Rising from the bench, Allison began to pace. "Don't laugh when I say this, but I'm a mess of tangled emotions."

Rosa grinned, and Allison stopped to shake her finger in mock reprimand.

"Sorry. But that is what I have been trying to tell you."

"You are always right, aren't you?"

"*Nein*, but trust me when I tell you I understand what you are going through." She patted Conrad's back. "I am listening."

Allison shrugged. "If you ask Chaz, he'll probably tell you we had a lovely time."

"I am more interested in what *you* think."

"In some respects, it was a delightful afternoon. We laughed and chatted about everything and nothing. Then we started talking about you and Basil, and your courtship. I commented that I never believed you were a Nazi, and that's when things took a turn for the worse. Chaz became nasty and vulgar."

She rubbed her forehead. "Then the storm blew in, and the skies opened and poured buckets of water on us. We sought shelter in the gazebo where Chaz's dark mood seemed to lift. We danced, and I think he was about to kiss me, but a clap of thunder startled us, and the moment passed. He apologized for being beastly. I told him about our agreement to pray for him, and he didn't seem to mind. But he thinks I'm doing all this as his friend. He seems to have no idea that I still love him." Her lower lip quivered, and she blinked back the tears that had formed in her eyes. "What is wrong with me? I've cried more in the last week than I have in months."

"You said it yourself. You are a girl in love."

Allison stopped pacing and flounced onto the bench. "What is your advice for this lovelorn woman?"

"We continue to pray. It has only been one day. God will show us the way." Her forehead wrinkled. "But you need to think about what life would be like with Chaz. Did he indicate whether or not he can expect his memory to return? When he became mean, did he get violent? Does his temper make him dangerous?"

"So many questions to consider." Allison shook her head. "His behavior didn't make me afraid, but his mood swings were a bit disconcerting." She smoothed her skirt. "You didn't say it outright, but I am running ahead of the Lord. I need to remember that he's going to work this out, and he'll help me through it."

"Waiting is the hard—"

"Mrs. Quincey?"

Molly, Rosa's housekeeper, stood at the garden gate. She held up an envelope. "I must beg your forgiveness. This came in the post today for Mr. Quincey, but I tucked it in my apron pocket and forgot all about it until just now."

Rosa extended her hand. "There is nothing to forgive."

"I won't let it happen again."

"Please, do not fret, Molly. This is not the terrible mistake you are making it out to be. Go inside and have a cup of tea. You will feel better."

"Yes. Thank you." The woman hurried back into the house.

Frowning, Rosa studied the ornate seal on the corner of the envelope.

Allison leaned over her shoulder. "The British embassy? Why would they be contacting Basil?"

"I do not know, and frankly I am afraid to ask him. I did not confront him about the time we saw him at the lake when he was supposed to be in London. He has been secretive lately. Closing the door to his office and making numerous telephone calls. He has also typed several things himself. Why would he do that when I have handled all the administrative needs since we married?"

"Perhaps he's giving you a break because of Conrad."

"That is just it. I have not had a break. I am continuing to type his correspondence and other documents, but there have been several instances when I have woken up to hear him typing in the office. What could be so confidential that he needs to type it in the dead of night?"

"This would make sense if we were still at war." Allison's eyes widened. "Could he still be involved with those activities?"

A tear trickled down Rosa's cheek. "After nearly four years of being his wife, there are times I feel that I do not really know him."

Chapter Eleven

The following morning, Chaz stood in front of Rosa's house. Despite the cool breeze, he perspired as if he had run an Olympic race. He rolled his shoulders, but his neck muscles remained taut. Blowing out a deep breath, he knocked on the gleaming cherry-wood door.

Footsteps sounded inside, and he stiffened his spine. What if Basil answered the door? How would he explain his need to see the man's wife?

The door opened, and Rosa appeared holding Conrad by the hand. She smiled and raised her eyebrows. "Chaz, it is lovely to see you. Basil is out in the back field. Do you know which one that is?"

"I'm here to speak with you." He yanked off his fedora and gripped it by the rim. "That is, if you have time to see me."

"Of course. Please come in." She lifted the little boy. Kissing his cheek, she asked, "Conrad-*liebchen*, can you say hello to Mr. Powell?"

The child frowned then hid his face.

Chaz grimaced. "My reputation precedes me."

"Nonsense." She smiled. "He is at a rather clingy stage. Do not take it personally." She led Chaz through the corridor into the kitchen where she pulled a chair out with her foot and set her son in it. Gesturing to the other chairs, she lowered herself into the seat nearest to Conrad. She slapped her forehead and rose again. "Forgive my lack of manners. May I get you some tea?"

"No, thank you. Please, sit."

Rosa dropped back into the chair. She pushed a pile of blank paper and a cracked teacup of crayons toward Conrad. His face lit up as he knelt on the seat and dumped the cup onto the table. Grabbing the red stick he began to scribble on the page.

She smiled and folded her hands. "That should give us a few minutes of peace. What would you like to discuss?"

"You and Allison seem to be close friends. Can I assume that Allison told you about our picnic? About my outburst?"

"We have no secrets from each other."

"I'll take that as a yes, which means I need to apologize for what I said. I was disrespectful about you to Allison, and for that I'm deeply sorry."

"Thank you, Chaz. It took courage to come over here, and I appreciate it. You have been through a terrible ordeal that I cannot understand. Allison told you we are praying for your recovery. It may not happen as you wish, but God will heal you."

"Dad said the same thing." He fiddled with the crease on his hat, then set it on the table and met her eyes. "He told me I accepted Christ as my Savior when I was a child, so I know I'm part of God's family even though I can't remember asking. And I'm praying, too, although most times it feels as if my words are bouncing off the ceiling. I have a long road ahead of me, and I vacillate between trust in God and terror of who this head injury and amnesia have made me."

Rosa squeezed his arm. "God hears you, Chaz, and he feels your pain. Remember that no one is out of the reach of God's forgiveness. You have not had a relationship with God since your accident, so you are a little rusty, but he is beside you, as he always was. He is welcoming you back, just as we are."

Chaz thumbed a stray tear from his eye. He straightened and swallowed past the lump in his throat. "I hope so; because I've realized, since spending time with Allison, that I have feelings for her. I may not remember our past relationship, but my heart is drawn to her in a way I can't explain. She's the last thing I think about at night and the first thing when I wake up in the morning. I find myself wondering what she's doing or where she is."

"Sounds serious."

"It is, but I don't want to saddle her with an invalid."

"Invalid? I do not wish to pry, but do you have other medical issues besides the headaches?"

"No, but doesn't that describe my condition?"

She shook her head. "I do not know what the doctors told you, but unless your loss of memory and headaches prevent you from retaining information, you should be able to learn a trade. You could support a wife and family."

"I don't want to hurt Allison." He hunched over the table. "What if I do something foolish, or selfish, or mean?"

Rosa laughed and covered her mouth for a moment. "Then you would be human like the rest of us."

He cocked his head. "I don't understand."

"Basil and I love each other very much, but we are not perfect. We make mistakes, or choose to put our own needs above those of the other, or say or do something spiteful. But the beautiful thing about our relationship is that God is part of it, and when we mess up, we ask his forgiveness and each other's."

"You make it sound easy."

"It is simple; however, it is far from easy. But it *is* worth the effort."

Chaz rose and stepped to the window, his back to Rosa. Did he have the right qualities to be the man he wanted to be? Could he get past his injuries and insecurities to pursue Allison like a normal suitor? Would she accept him if he did? After initial resistance, she had melted into his arms during their dance in the gazebo. Was she just being a friend as she claimed, or did she still have feelings for him? Was he willing to risk his own heart to find out?

With a deep sigh, he turned to Rosa. "Perhaps it's best if I walk away from this relationship."

Chapter Twelve

"Have you been able to definitively pinpoint their location? This plan must be executed without fail."

Basil's voice. Allison sucked in a breath and crouched behind the hulking John Deere tractor in Basil's barn. Who was he talking to?

"*Nein,* but I have a man making final inquiries with the authorities as we speak. I should be able to confirm the information for you this week."

A German accent? Rosa suspected her husband was involved in some sort of secret operation. Did this conversation with a German man prove her correct? Was the operation legal?

"Can we trust their government to give us the truth?"

"That part of Germany is still too unstable to be sure of anything. That is why my man is double checking his facts."

Pressing a hand against her mouth to stifle her gasp, Allison sagged. What could Basil possibly be doing with anyone in Germany? Who was the German? She shifted to peer through the machinery, but could only glimpse the men's legs.

"This has dragged on too long. If we don't act soon they could move, and we'd have to start the search all over again."

"Yes, sir. I understand your urgency, but we must be discreet. My fellow countrymen do not take kindly to foreigners nosing about. The war may be over, but distrust and hostility does not heal overnight."

"I've paid a lot of money to make this happen. Don't disappointment me."

"Yes, Mr. Quincey. I will be in touch."

"See that you are."

Footsteps receded. Allison raised herself above the tractor, then dropped to the ground. Basil remained inside. How long would he be there? Rosa knew Allison had ventured into the barn. Would she come looking for her and give away her presence?

Bumps and clangs sounded as Basil rummaged around the barn.

Would he never leave?

More footsteps sounded indicating the presence of another person. Allison bit her lip.

"Mr. Quincey, I need your opinion about the potato crop in the lower field."

"I'll be with you straightaway, James, but I've something to tie up in here first."

"Do you need my assistance?"

"No, wait for me in the field."

"Very good."

The men left the barn, and silence descended. Several minutes passed. Allison stood and rubbed the cramps from her thighs. Grabbing the basket she spied on the top shelf, she rushed out the door.

"In a hurry, Allison?"

She whipped her head toward the voice. Basil emerged from behind one of the fourteen-foot-high hay bales near the building.

"Basil! Er…yes. Rosa asked me to cut some flowers so she could make an arrangement for the dinner table."

"You heard my conversation with Johann. Why did you not identify yourself?"

His face was a mask.

"I…uh…" She shrugged. "I don't know. It happened so fast. Once I realized you were discussing a secret plan, I became frightened. Especially after Rosa and I saw you at the pond when you were supposed to be in London. And she showed me the envelope from the embassy." She squared her shoulders. "What are you involved in, Basil? I thought you were a Christian. I won't have you hurt Rosa. She deserves better than your duplicity."

He threw back his head and laughed long and hard. She stared at him. What was so funny about this situation? Did he have no feelings at all?

"I'm glad you think this is amusing, but I'd like an answer. Rosa deserves an explanation."

Basil grinned and wiped his eyes. "My apologies for laughing. Your loyalty to my wife is gratifying—she couldn't ask for a better friend—but you've misunderstood my intentions and my 'involvement', as you put it."

"Then explain yourself. Because right now, it sounds as if you're nosing about the German government for some nefarious reason."

Chuckling, Basil shook his head. "You've been reading Graham Greene again, haven't you?"

"Is that your way of telling me you're not part of the British Secret Service, nor are you spying on Germany?"

"I'm going to correct your imaginative theory, but you must swear to me that you'll keep all of this to yourself. Agreed?"

"How can I agree to that? I still don't know if what you're doing is above board."

"Because I am a Christian, and I wouldn't do anything underhanded to compromise my relationship with God." He cocked his head. "I'm disappointed you could think I would do something deceitful and illegal."

"I must say I was stunned when the conversation seemed to point to that conclusion. Forgive me for assuming the worst."

He waved his hand in a dismissive gesture. "I'm sure your love for Rosa colors your opinion. You saw how some of the Land Army girls treated her during the war. Now, do you agree to my terms?"

"Absolutely."

"Good, because you're going to be pleased with the news." He looked over his shoulder then back at Allison. Lowering his voice, he winked. "Can't let our girl hear any of this. You know Rosa left her parents behind when she immigrated to England with Noreen. After the war, she sent them a letter, but they never responded, so she assumes they're dead. There was no record of their deaths, and I have some advantageous contacts, so I made several attempts to find them. Unfortunately, until now, those searches have been unsuccessful."

"But you've discovered their whereabouts. Pinpointed their location is what you said."

"I'm guardedly optimistic. We've had false leads before, but I feel God is telling me our search is over. Once we determine whether the couple we found is Rosa's mother and father, we'll provide the necessary arrangements for them to leave the country."

"You make it sound difficult."

"It is. They are in the section of Germany that is controlled by the Soviets. I'm not at liberty to share the reports I've been given about what's happening there. Suffice it to say, there have been numerous distasteful incidents."

"Is it dangerous?"

His face grim, he nodded. "Very dangerous. Her parents' lives could be in jeopardy if they remain under Soviet jurisdiction. Now do you see why I can't share any of this with Rosa? She'd be devastated if she thought her parents had survived only to be lost during the transition."

"Forgive my hasty conclusions about your activities. I've never seen a man love a woman like you do. You'd sacrifice everything for Rosa, wouldn't you?"

"She deserves nothing less." He crossed his arms. "But I'm not the only man capable of this kind of love. Rosa and I have been talking about you and Chaz. She thinks he loves you like that. He did before the war, and he still does, but he's afraid of hurting you." He pulled out his pocket watch and glanced at it before tucking it away. "I've got to meet James at one of the fields, but you already know that."

Flushing, Allison giggled. "Yes. By the way, how did you know I was in the barn?"

He flicked at the feather tucked under the ribbon on her hat. "I saw that poking up from behind the John Deere. If you're going to eavesdrop, next time take off your fedora."

"Oh, bother."

He winked at her, then turned and strode toward the fields, whistling as he walked.

Allison bent and retrieved the basket from the ground. Was Basil right? Did Chaz still love her? Could she break through the barrier of fear that surrounded him?

"God help me, I do love him." She set her jaw and headed for the flower gardens. "Unless you tell me differently, Lord, I'm going to court him." Giggling, she said, "He doesn't stand a chance."

Chapter Thirteen

Allison's pulse stuttered. She glanced at the watch pinned to her bodice and grimaced. Basil was late. He should have arrived with Rosa's parents more than an hour ago. The living room was filled with friends who chatted and laughed with abandon. Basil had arranged for the church's monthly potluck to be held at his home. None of the guests knew the real reason for the party.

Ten days had passed since she confronted Basil about his secretive behavior. Ten days filled with a roller coaster of emotions. Rosa's mother and father had been whisked out of Germany and were on their way to England when Rosa's mother had fallen gravely ill and was rushed to a hospital in France.

Only yesterday a telegram arrived with the news she had recovered, and the two were on their way once more. After crossing the

Channel from Le Havre to Portsmouth they would catch the train. A difficult journey for those in good health, the trip would be arduous for the elderly couple.

In addition to worrying about Rosa's parents, Allison had executed her plan to woo Chaz. Another picnic, a bicycle ride around the village, sightseeing trips to Greenwich and Putney, and a day at the beach in Hastings seemed to have helped him release some of his anger and frustration. He was experiencing fewer mood swings and had not had any during their day at the beach.

Regularly asking her to pray with him, he shared that he was finally at a place where he realized God hadn't caused his amnesia as some sort of awful prank or punishment and was prepared to live without his memories of the past.

Yesterday, she caught him staring at her, and he grinned like the Cheshire Cat then gave her a swift hug before claiming he had a surprise for her. She begged him for a hint, but he refused, saying she'd find out soon enough.

Smiling, Allison checked her watch again. A mere three minutes had passed. What if something had gone wrong? *Lord, please keep them safe. Rosa deserves this happiness. She's done so much for others.*

On the far side of the room, Rosa bustled around the food table clearing soiled dishes and wiping up drips on the table cloth. She looked up and smiled at Allison.

Threading her way through the crowd, Allison arrived at Rosa's side. "I'd offer to help, but you'll only tell me to enjoy myself. I could say the same to you, but I know you are quite happy at the moment."

"You know me well, *ja*. It does give me joy to open my home and make things pretty." Rosa gestured to the guests. "Most of these people have very little. They made it through the war, but few did as well as Basil. We need to share from our bounty."

"Basil is a lucky man, Rosa. I hope he realizes that."

Rosa blushed. "He tells me every day how blessed he is that God put us together." She sobered. "I still have not approached him about what he is doing. I have been praying, and strangely enough, God has given me peace. The situation must not be as it appears."

Allison shook her head. "I'd not be as accepting."

A knock sounded, and the door swung open. Allison and Rosa turned. The church organist and her husband entered the room. Allison's stomach clenched. Where was Basil?

The woman held up a towel-wrapped bundle of food. "Sorry to be late. We had to stop for petrol, and there was a queue. I thought we'd never get here."

Rosa hastened to the entrance and relieved the woman of her dish. "No apology necessary. Make yourself at home. It is lovely that you could join us."

Footsteps sounded on the steps outside, and Allison held her breath. Surely that was Basil.

As if her thoughts conjured him up, he appeared in the doorway. Allison's gaze shot to his face, and he gave her an imperceptible nod. Grinning, he swept Rosa into his arms, the dish pressed between them. "I've missed you, wife."

She giggled and swatted at him with her empty hand. "Basil, what are you doing? We have guests."

"I know, my dear, I invited them. Now, give that dish to someone because I've brought you a surprise, and you'll need both hands."

The buzz of conversation ceased, and people turned to watch.

Allison rushed forward and grabbed the bundle. She caught sight of Chaz on the porch, and he sent her a dazzling smile. Her breath caught.

Basil wrapped one arm around Rosa's waist and covered her eyes with the other. "Chaz, are you ready?"

"Ready."

"Basil—"

"Hush, darling, it will be worth the wait."

———————————◆———————————

Chaz led a white-haired couple through the door. They stopped in front of Rosa, tears coursing down their cheeks. He swallowed against the lump in his throat.

Uncovering Rosa's eyes, Basil whispered into her ear, "Surprise."

Rosa gasped and fell into her parents' arms. The three of them cried, and their German words tumbled over each other.

Meeting Allison's eyes over the sobbing trio Chaz tipped his head toward the door. She plunked the dish on the food table and weaved through the crowd. He held out his arm, and she tucked her hand in the crook of his elbow as they slipped outside. Descending the porch, they sauntered across the grassy lawn.

"Rosa must be beside herself with happiness. It was nice of you to help Basil pull off the surprise."

"Listening to your stories about all he has done for Rosa, I've learned a lot about sacrificial love. He seems to be an amazing man of God. He would do anything for Rosa, even walk straight into danger. His connection had to dissuade him from flying directly to Germany himself."

"I saw his integrity and bravery during the war."

Chaz led her to a stone bench under the wild cherry tree not far from the house. They seated themselves, and Chaz turned her toward him. He cradled her hands in his. His pulse quickened.

"Allison, it's been a difficult few weeks since I've returned, and you've been nothing but kind to me. I've been alternately beastly and distant. Your prayers and support in light of my behavior speak of your gracious, Godly nature. I don't deserve your friendship."

"Chaz—"

He put his finger on her lips for a moment. "Let me finish, or I might lose my nerve."

She nodded, and he stroked her cheek. He felt her shiver at his touch.

"I love you, Allison. I can't remember anything about our past relationship, but I don't need to. I see the woman you are, and I can't help but love you. You may never care for me as you once did, but would you be willing to start over? To allow me to court you as you deserve? I don't know what the future holds for me or my recovery, but I don't want to face it without you by my side."

"I love you, too, Chaz. I've never stopped. God will see us through whatever happens."

Her face glowed, and he pulled her to her feet, drawing her toward him. Staring into her eyes, he bent and dropped a gentle kiss on her mouth.

His lips tingled at her touch, and his heart skipped a beat before settling into rhythm with hers.

Epilogue

May, 1946

Allison twirled in front of the mirror, and her ivory wedding gown rustling around her legs. She met Rosa's eyes in their reflection and smiled. "Here we are again."

Rosa hugged her from behind. "God is good, *ja?*"

"I still pinch myself to make sure I'm not dreaming. You must feel the same way, being reunited with your parents."

"Basil told me everything and apologized for his need to deceive me. He promised never to do so again. *Mutti* and *Vati* love him and are settling in nicely. They miss their friends, but Mr. and Mrs. Deming from church have taken them under their wing."

"Then they shall feel at home in no time."

Pressing her hand against her middle, Allison took a shaky breath. "It's as if mice are tap dancing inside me."

"I felt the same way at my own wedding. *Mutti* Noreen claimed it was normal. Once you walk up the aisle and see Chaz, your nerves will disappear."

A rap sounded at the door before it opened. Basil poked his head into the room. "Is there a bride in the house?" He grinned and pointed to his watch. "Time's a-wasting, my girl. You mustn't leave your groom standing at the altar. Last I saw him, he looked as if he might faint dead away."

Allison grinned at him as she curtsied then pulled her veil over her face. "Ready as I'll ever be. We don't want the poor man to pass out. As least not before he completes his vows."

Rosa chortled and pushed past Basil. "Give me two minutes, then bring her out when you hear the music."

Basil nodded and held out his arm. "You're a beautiful bride, Allison. Chaz is blessed to have you in his life."

She picked up her bouquet filled with miniature roses and Queen Anne's lace. "Thank you for giving me away, Basil."

"You're very welcome. I'm sure this is a bittersweet day for you without your parents. The war took too many too soon."

She blinked away her tears. "I'd like to believe they're watching from heaven."

The strains of the violins filtered toward them, and Allison gripped Basil's arm as they made their way outside into the sunshine. Chairs had been set up in the meadow behind the house. A wooden arbor draped with white muslin nestled under a mammoth beech tree, and a crystal vase filled with a rainbow of blossoms stood on a table to the right of the vicar.

The guests rose and turned toward her. Their images blurred as she traversed the plush, green lawn of the aisle. Chaz's handsome face, with a broad smile and bright eyes, came into view. Warmth filled her.

She arrived at the front, and the vicar motioned for the congregation to seat themselves. Basil placed her hand in Chaz's then sat next to Rosa.

"We are gathered today to join this man and this woman…"

Allison sighed. *Thank you, God.*

The End

What did you think of *A Love Not Forgotten?*

Thank you so much for purchasing *A Love Not Forgotten*. You could have selected any number of books to read, but you chose this book.

I hope it added encouragement and exhortation to your life. If so, it would be nice if you could share this book with your family and friends by posting to Facebook (www.facebook.com) and/or Twitter (www.twitter.com).

If you enjoyed this book and found some benefit in reading it, I'd appreciate it if you could take some time to post a review on Amazon, Goodreads, Kobo, GooglePlay, Apple Books, or other book review site of your choice. Your feedback and support will help me to improve my writing craft for future projects and make this book even better.

Thank you again for your purchase.

Blessings,

Linda Shenton Matchett

Acknowledgments

Although writing a book is a solitary task, it is not a solitary journey. There have been many who have helped and encouraged me along the way.

My parents, Richard and Jean Shenton, who presented me with my first writing tablet and encouraged me to capture my imagination with words. Thanks, Mom and Dad!

Scribes212 – my ACFW online critique group: Valerie Goree, Marcia Lahti, and the late Loretta Boyett (passed on to Glory, but never forgotten). Without your input, my writing would not be nearly as effective.

Eva Marie Everson – my mentor/instructor with Christian Writers' Guild. You took a timid, untrained student and turned her into a writer. Many thanks!

SincNE, and the folks who coordinate the Crimebake Writing Conference. I have attended many writing conferences, but without a doubt, Crimebake is one of the best. The workshops, seminars, panels, critiques, and every tiny aspect are well-executed, professional, and educational.

Special thanks to Hank Phillippi Ryan, Halle Ephron, and Roberta Isleib for your encouragement and spot-on critiques of my work.

Thanks to my Book Brigade who provide information, encouragement, and support.

A heartfelt thank you to my brothers, Jack Shenton and Douglas Shenton, and my sister, Susan Shenton Greger for being enthusiastic cheerleaders during my writing journey. Your support means more than you'll know.

My husband, Wes, deserves special kudos for understanding my need to write. Thank you for creating my writing room – it's perfect, and I'm thankful for it every day. Thank you for your willingness to accept a house that's a bit cluttered, laundry that's not always done, and meals on the go. I love you.

And finally, to God be the glory. I thank Him for giving me the gift of writing and the inspiration to tell stories that shine the light on His goodness and mercy.

Read on for the first chapter in *Love's Harvest*, Book one in the Wartime Bride series; retellings of biblical stories set during WWII.

Volga Region, Russia, 1923

Chapter One

"We'll die if we don't leave this place. Pack only what you can carry." Edmund Hirsch poked his bony arms into the sleeves of his wool coat that sported more holes than Swiss cheese. A paroxysm of coughing gripped his body, the result of a mustard gas attack on his German platoon nine years ago during The Great War.

After several minutes the coughing ceased, and he mopped the sweat from his forehead with a dingy, gray handkerchief. "Be ready. We set out tomorrow at first light."

"Where will we go, *Vati*?" Five-year-old Conrad's voice trembled.

"Don't be a baby, Conrad." Older by two minutes, Conrad's twin brother, Manfred, finished tying his boot laces and jumped off the chair, his shoes clomping against the bare wood floor. His bright blue eyes blazed above his hollow cheeks.

"Hush, children." Noreen stroked Conrad's white-blond hair and met her husband's terse look with one of her own. "You heard your father. There's no time to waste."

❖

Noreen yanked the zipper closed on her over-stuffed canvas satchel. Always resourceful, Edmund had attached straps to the moss-green bag so she could wear it on her back. She would also carry a suitcase in each hand. The journey promised to be arduous.

Sighing, she wiped a weary hand across her dry eyes. Even if she had any tears remaining, crying was useless. It would not make their situation less dire.

Muted voices and the occasional bump filtered through the ceiling from the boys' bedroom above. Noreen shivered and hunched into her threadbare, ruby-red sweater. An impulse purchase made during her honeymoon, the garment held more memories than warmth. Edmund insisted it brought out the roses in her cheeks.

She tossed the bulging satchel to the floor and turned her attention to the yawning luggage on the bed. Two steel pots and a fry pan nestled in the bottom of one boxy, brown suitcase between faded blue towels that had been a belated wedding present from her mother and father.

Hopefully, Edmund would find somewhere they could live in his home country with enough food to actually cook. Here, along the Volga River in Russia, the crops had failed again, and the famine was entering its second year. The decision whether to eat or plant their seed wheat had caused many families to die of starvation.

Shuffling footsteps sounded behind her. She turned as Edmund enveloped her in his arms. Nestling against his too-thin chest, she breathed in his musky scent. He bent and kissed her forehead, his black beard scraping her skin.

"You work too hard." He tucked a stray strand of her nutmeg-colored hair behind her ear.

She leaned into his touch. "Isn't that why you married me?"

"No, *Schatzi,* it is most certainly not." He grinned. "You stole my heart. I had to marry you, or I would die a broken man."

"Don't joke about that. Our friends are dying every day." She frowned. "Who knew this famine would last so long? If it weren't for the bit of help arriving from America's Volga Relief Society, matters would be much worse."

"They are sending more assistance than we are receiving. Jakob told me there is proof the government is confiscating some of the packages and keeping the money to construct new buildings and conduct repairs. As always, development of the country is valued above the lives of the people."

"Shhh!" She pressed the work-worn fingers of her right hand against his lips. "You could get in trouble for saying that. Then where would we be?"

Edmund hugged her. "There is no one to hear us, but I understand your fear. Many unexplained disappearances make for extreme caution." He released her and gestured toward the pile of clothes on their bed. "Enough depressing talk. What can I do to help?"

"Do you have our passports? With the government ratcheting up the price, we have no more savings to purchase new ones."

"Now who's speaking out against the authorities?" He patted the breast pocket of his coat. "I have the passports and our traveling papers safe and sound."

"Good." Noreen waved him away. "Then go see what the boys are about. I gave explicit instructions about what to pack, but they have a mind of their own." She shook her head. "Well, Manfred does. Conrad simply tags along."

He kissed the tip of her nose and raised his hand in mock salute. "*Jawohl!*"

She giggled and pushed him out of the room. Closing the door behind him, she sobered and dropped to her knees next to the bed. "Dear Heavenly Father, thank You for Edmund. He is a good man. Give him strength for the journey and keep us safe as we travel. Soften the hearts of his family so they will welcome us home."

Home.

Berlin was Edmund's home. Not hers.

English born and bred, Noreen stroked the floral bedspread as visions of daffodils in Regents Park flitted through her head, their golden yellow blooms swaying in the breeze. Big Ben soaring into the sky. Tower Bridge spanning the River Thames. Pristine white swans fishing the waters of Serpentine Lake in Hyde Park where a chance meeting changed the trajectory of her life.

In an effort to heal his damaged lungs, Edmund moved to London after the war. Someone told him the damp English air would act as a balm. A lover of art, he had attended the Spring Festival where she sat under a tent selling her baskets.

She climbed to her feet, and her gaze sought out the willow basket on their dresser. The basket Edmund purchased when he returned to her booth after taking his girlfriend home. His last date with the woman.

Noreen's smile broadened. Who knew basket weaving would catch her a husband? She flushed as she remembered the conversation.

"If I purchase this basket, will you go out with me?"

"What about your girlfriend?"

"I told her we were finished, that I was going to marry you."

"Isn't that a bit rash? You don't even know me."

"I know enough."

After a whirlwind courtship, Edmund asked for her hand in marriage. Her parents objected, so Edmund took her to the register office where he wed her in front of two gray-haired, bored-looking clerks. A year later the twins were born, and her parents decided being grandparents was more important than holding a grudge. They eventually grew to love their German son-in-law as much as their daughter did. Enough to support the family's move to Russia in another effort to heal Edmund's lungs. She swallowed against the lump in her throat. Her parents' death last year in a train accident still stung.

Overheard, a thump followed by laughter broke her reverie. Warmth filled her. She loved her country, but she loved Edmund more. That is why she would leave all but her most necessary possessions and travel to yet another foreign country to live with her in-laws. People she had never met who spoke a language she didn't know.

Other Titles

Romance

Love's Harvest, Wartime Brides, Book 1

Love's Rescue, Wartime Brides, Book 2

Love's Belief, Wartime Brides, Book 3

Love's Allegiance, Wartime Brides, Book 4

Love Found in Sherwood Forest

On the Rails

A Doctor in the House (The Hope of Christmas Collection)

Mystery

Under Fire

Under Ground

Under Cover

Murder of Convenience, Women of Courage, Book 1

Non-Fiction

WWII Word Find, Volume 1

Linda Shenton Matchett writes about ordinary people who did extraordinary things in days gone by. She is a volunteer docent and archivist at the Wright Museum of WWII and a trustee for her local public library. Born in Baltimore, Maryland, a stone's throw from Fort McHenry, she has lived in historical places most of her life. Now located in central New Hampshire, Linda's favorite activities include exploring historic sites and immersing herself in the imaginary worlds created by other authors.

Website/blog: http://www.LindaShentonMatchett.com

Facebook: http://www.facebook.com/LindaShentonMatchettAuthor

Pinterest: http://www.pinterest.com/lindasmatchett

Amazon: https://www.amazon.com/Linda-Shenton-Matchett/e/B01DNB54S0

Goodreads: http://www.goodreads.com/author_linda_matchett

Bookbub: http://www.bookbub.com/authors/linda-shenton-matchett